THE
PATCHWORK PRINCESS

ADVENTURES OF RA-ME,
THE TRAVELING TROUBADOUR-BOOK 1

CONNIE S. ARNOLD

THE PATCHWORK PRINCESS
ADVENTURES OF RA-ME, THE TRAVELING TROUBADOUR-BOOK 1

iUniverse books may be ordered through booksellers or by contacting:

iUniverse
1663 Liberty Drive
Bloomington, IN 47403
www.iuniverse.com
1-800-Authors (1-800-288-4677)

ISBN: 978-1-5320-5615-4 (sc)
ISBN: 978-1-5320-6059-5 (hc)
ISBN: 978-1-5320-5616-1 (e)

Library of Congress Control Number: 2018912131

Print information available on the last page.

iUniverse rev. date: 11/26/2018

Dedicated to my three grandchildren:

Sarah, and the twins, Spencer and Tyler

THE PATCHWORK PRINCESS

You say it's my turn, Falstaff? I can do it, and that's for sure. O. K., I'll begin. Everyone gather near.

Once upon a time... Oh, I know, that isn't an original beginning, but it did happen only once, and I had quite a time.

Falstaff and I are boon companions, but for those of you staying in this inn tonight who don't know me, my name is Ra-me—you know as in do-re-mi-fa-so-la-ti-do. I am a freelance minstrel and traveling troubadour. The things that have happened to me!

Ah, I know, Falstaff, I'm wandering from my story. Yes, it's a new one. Of course, it's true; I know that skeptical look of yours.

Anyway, I got an invitation to play in the king's castle in the Parkingham Kingdom. I can tell you I jumped at the chance to play at that castle. It would be good for my career. Besides, I had heard that he had three beautiful daughters.

You weren't in the village at the time, Falstaff, but when the king's messenger rode up to my parents' humble cottage, you can imagine the excitement.

The invitation from King Lister of Parkingham was announcing the marriage of his eldest daughter. I was to be there in a fortnight prepared to entertain.

Truly, Falstaff, if you'd been here I would have asked you to accompany me. It's a long ride to Parkingham.

Well, I got busy. I polished my harp, restrung my lute, packed my silken blouses and breeches, saddled Roscoe and started my journey early two days hence. I passed the time to good advantage. I wrote poems of love and set them to music and practiced my art as I rode.

It was afternoon the day I came within sight of the castle. The glowing red sun turned the walls a soft pink, and a white cloud encircled the highest turret. The blue sky made a fantasy background for it all. Ah, Falstaff, you should have been with me.

As I neared the castle, I spied a large wooden sign fastened between two trees back away from the road. There was a path from the road that led to the sign. I was curious, so I went to see what the sign said.

The little path was well-traveled and the ground was completely bare in front of the sign from the many footprints. They had come on foot and on horseback to read the sign. It read:

King Lister of Parkingham happily announces the marriage of his eldest daughter, Princess Ina, to the brave knight who will rescue her from Terrance the Terrible's ten-story tower.

Besides my daughter's hand in marriage, further reward will include one-third of my kingdom, 3 bags of gold, 3 new suits of armor, 3 white steeds, and a sword with a ruby-studded hilt.

Now, Falstaff, you know I like a bag of gold as well as the next man, but I'm not greedy. I didn't feel moved to volunteer for the position as King Lister's son-in-law, but I can tell you I began to have a fear about my invitation to perform. I had traveled a long way, and it was a long way back. I needed the job. I didn't want anything to upset this engagement; and my engagement, it seemed, depended upon Princess Ina's engagement.

Roscoe and I finished the journey to the castle at a slow walk. Roscoe's hoofs made loud, knocking sounds as he carried me across the drawbridge and a groom ran to meet us and took hold of Roscoe's bridle.

"Are you Ra-me, the much-lauded troubadour?" he called to me. I nodded yes, and he continued. "You are just in time. King Lister is anxiously waiting. I will take you to him." He showed me a doorway to enter, and he led Roscoe away.

King Lister was the shape of a pear, and his short beard bristled excitedly as he talked. I knelt respectfully, one knee resting on the highly polished floor of the throne room.

"Rise, Troubadour," he cried out to me. "Your ballads will soon be sung." He flung out a hand in a grand gesture toward an open window. "Even now a brave knight has ridden out to bring back Princess Ina. Happiness will soon descend upon us all."

I was puzzled. Only the King showed any joy. His servants wore somber faces and their shoulders sagged.

"Milord, shall I sing for you now?" I asked King Lister.

"Save your voice, Troubadour. The day after tomorrow we shall have a celebration. I know it."

He turned his back on us all and went to look out the window. Falstaff, I do believe he was expecting to see that brave knight riding into the courtyard with Princess Ina safely back within his fold. As far as King Lister knew now, we had vanished.

"Are you the singer of songs that our father, the King, has hired?"

I thought I'd died and gone to heaven, men. The sound of her voice was as sweet as an angel's song. The gold of her hair shamed the sun, and her eyes were the velvet blue of morning glories. Her skin blushed healthy as a rose, and her full lips were luscious as cherries.

When her beauty had me on the verge of a swoon, I heard another voice. "Oh, is the troubadour here, sister?"

The husky, richness of this voice caused an icy sensation at the base of my spine. This vision had hair like midnight cascading in waves down her back, her eyes were well-cut jades fringed with thick, black lashes. Her smile held me bewitched.

"I am Princess Rowena, and this is my sister, Princess Annabella." Never have I bowed more fervently over any other hands.

"Please call me Ra-me," I introduced myself. They could have called "Hey there, varlet," and I would have answered gladly.

I think of my fate as being sealed that evening, unknown to me.

There was a lavish feast prepared for the evening meal, and I was invited to eat with the court. But, alas, I sat between a dream and a vision, and my heart was in my throat challenging any but the smallest morsel of food.

Perhaps, it piqued me a little, but I couldn't help but notice the many knights that were also guests of King Lister. They were all suitors that had tried to rescue Princess Ina and failed in their attempt. I supposed they were resting up to try again.

Two knights, Sir Edward and Sir Charles, seemed to have forgotten Princess Ina entirely and were bent on entertaining Princess Annabella and Princess Rowena with their wit and flattering words, and the princesses weren't as inattentive as I would've liked.

"Would you go for a stroll in the garden before retiring, Ra-me?" The dulcet tones of Princess Rowena floated to me. I, of course, would have walked off a ledge into a viper's nest had she suggested it.

"I could think of nothing more pleasant," I agreed. It did me no harm to see the pained expression on Sir Edward's long face.

The heavy scent of honeysuckle had a drugging effect, and the moon cast a spell of its own. I was lost before I began.

"You have no idea how it shatters us to have our dear, dear sister in the clutches of Terrance the Terrible," she told me. In the moonlight, her face was an oval pearl, and I thought a crystal sparkled at me from her cheek. She continued, "And, I cannot marry, nor my sister Annabella, until she is wed. Princess Ina is eldest."

Like the Court fool, I talked too much. "What can I do to help?"

She extended her hand with a little moan of delight, "Oh, good sir, perhaps you can. If this last knight fails, we will work out a plan."

I slept the sleep of the innocent that night with visions of happily-ever-after in my brain accompanied by the scent of honeysuckle and moonlight coming in through my chamber window. I slept deep and long for the journey to Parkingham had been a tiring one.

The next morning, I was met by Princess Annabella. Sir Charles was just a few steps behind her. When she completely ignored that brave knight to give her attention solely to me, I gained about two inches in stature in my own eyes.

She had a delicious idea of a picnic on the green by the waterfall in the palace garden. I took my lute and serenaded Princess Annabella, my voice rich with feeling and my heart throbbing with love. Sunbeams danced on the gold coils of her hair, and her eyes stole the fathomless blue of the deep stream. She gazed at me enraptured, I thought, as I sang in hushed, reverent tones.

"Dear Ra-me," she began. "How good of you to volunteer to help our poor, dear sister Princess Ina. I cannot marry until she is safely restored to our father and in the state of wedded bliss to the brave knight who rescues her."

How would I choose? The beauty of the day against the mystery of the night. Gold against a black pearl. Fate should never bring such a choice to bear upon a poor, mortal man.

"Your servant, Princess Annabella," I vowed.

That night as I lay upon my bed, I heard a commotion in the courtyard. Looking out from my window, I saw a knight on a giant steed gallop into the midst of a group of men. They helped him dismount, and they talked together. The laughter was riotous. Poor knight. I presumed they were making fun of his failure, for this was the last brave knight that rode out in an attempt to rescue Princess Ina.

The die was cast. My sword, my life, my honor was pledged to the rescue of Princess Ina. In the exuberance of youth, I looked forward to the morning light.

King Lister was delighted that I offered to ride out with Sir Charles and aid him in his second rescue attempt.

My resolve was strong. I would aid Sir Charles in freeing Princess Ina, but I would look forward to the freedom of her two beautiful sisters. It would be a hard choice, but I could not lose.

We didn't talk as we rode along. I supposed he was contemplating the seriousness of the task before him. My legs were sore from the long journey to Parkingham, so I hoped that the ten-story tower belonging to Terrance the Terrible wouldn't be too much further. The saddle wasn't as comfortable as the benches in the King's garden.

"What is our plan of attack?" Sir Charles asked me.

That was unexpected. This brave knight surely knew more about battle than a troubadour.

But he continued, "I failed shamefully the first time. I humbly ask your advice."

This did nothing to make me remember my lowly position.

"Sir Charles, I will fall in with your plan." I had no plan of my own.

"Ra-me, let me go in plain sight to the front of the tower and face Terrance the Terrible. While I am challenging him, you go into the tower through the back entrance, rescue Princess Ina, and ride safely toward the castle. I will catch up with you."

I nodded, not trusting my voice. Why was I here? A performer of ballads and composer of songs was in no way equipped to do battle. I thought about the two lovely princesses awaiting my return and my choice, and I took new courage.

The tower rose gray and plain before us, its stone walls marked at nine intervals with small square windows. I thought I saw a flutter of cloth from the top window. We pulled up our horses and surveyed the situation.

"This is as far as I got on my first attempt," Sir Charles' voice was grave but unafraid. "The dragon roared and the flames that came from his mouth frightened my brave steed, and he unseated me. And, alas, on foot I was unable to defeat the dragon and was forced to flee for my life."

I saw no signs of the dragon and breathed a sigh of relief.

"Are you ready, Sir Troubadour?" Sir Charles bestowed knighthood with great affect.

"Ready." I didn't recognize the courage in my own voice.

I didn't look back once I started galloping around to the back side of the tower. I could hear no other noise than that of my heartbeat in rhythm with the hoofbeats of my steed.

I dropped the reins, dismounted, and opened the heavy oak door which was, fortunately, unlocked. The hinges were smoothly oiled, and it made no sound.

I could feel the cold of the stone steps through the thin leather of my slippers, but my footfalls made no sound. I didn't even pause to look out the windows as I made my way up, up the spiral stairs to the chamber at the top of the tower.

"Your highness?" I whispered softly into the shadowy chamber. I could see a figure sitting, unmoving, in a chair.

"At last," she breathed. Her voice was like the third harmony of a trio. But as she stepped toward me, the revealing light from the window told me why Princess Ina had not been rescued before.

She looked like her sisters, that was for sure, but she looked like both of them, depending on the direction from which you viewed her. Her thick hair was parted in the middle further accentuating the shocking demarcation. On the right side, the tresses of hair were even more golden than those of Annabella's; on the left, the locks were more lustrous than the blue-black of a raven's wing. Both eyes were wide with expectation, but the right one rivaled the morning glory, and the left one soft as sable. Her dainty brows and thick sooty lashes helped pull her face together. Really, she was quite lovely when one got over the shock, but it was no great surprise that she would be considered anything but a "fair" damsel in distress when compared to Annabella and Rowena.

"You have been duped, kind sir. I watched your friend ride off as soon as you were out of sight. I will not blame you if you turn and flee. Now, you are left alone to rescue me," her voice was sad.

"Duped, your highness? It is an honor to rescue you from this 10-story tower of Terrance the Terrible. Where is that black knight?" I was only a little frightened. Maybe he'd kill me.

"He only visits the tower in the evenings to bring me food, so he won't be here for hours yet. I'm afraid he abducted me in the dark and thought I was my sister, Rowena," she confessed.

"And the dragon?" I asked. My voice was trembling.

"The dragon is hiding, because he is afraid now. His fire has gone out, and he can only spit ashes. Will you take me home?"

"But, Princess Ina, why wouldn't I take you back to King Lister?" I asked, pretending innocence. "It isn't every day a lowly troubadour gets the opportunity to rescue a fair damsel in distress."

"But, sir troubadour..."

"Ra-me, please..."

"Ra-me, can't you see that I am not beautiful. I am called the patchwork princess. If you take me back, my father will command that you marry me. My sisters are desperate for me to marry."

A shaft pierced my heart, but I would be gallant.

"It will be my honor, Princess Ina, if you will have me." I had a plan which was a wild gamble, but it was my only hope.

"You are a true knight, Ra-me." Happiness lit up her features.

"May I help you prepare to leave?"

"I have but a few things to take back," she said. "But I must tidy my hair."

"Let me help," I offered.

"You?" She was aghast.

"I had an older sister who loved for me to dress her hair," I told her. Remember my sister, Falstaff? She is bald.

I released the thick coils of her hair, the gold on the right and the ebony on the left. Artfully, I arranged her hair in an elaborate coiffure that entwined those two colors of hair into a masterful meeting of noon and midnight.

There was nothing I could do about the eyes, but they were nicely shaped and not crossed. She was a sweet little thing, and if my ruse failed, I supposed I could do worse.

We were met with cheers. The loyal subjects of King Lister lined up along the road leading to the castle. Sir Charles had made everyone aware that I was coming in with Princess Ina.

I smiled and waved to everyone. Princess Ina was so happy to be home that she was radiant. King Lister was so excited that he instantly invited everyone to a banquet in my honor that very night.

Everyone in Parkingham attended. I have never seen so many brave knights gathered in one place before. The tables groaned with the load of food—fruit, meats, pastries, vegetables from the King's own gardens.

Halfway through the banquet, King Lister rose and immediately all noise ceased. "I have promised my Princess Ina to the brave man who would rescue her. And so, it shall be. Would Ra-me, the brave troubadour, want to say a few words to us?"

This was the moment I had been waiting for. All afternoon in my room I had worked feverishly on the lyrics for the ballad I would perform tonight.

Never had the tones of my lute been more wonderful. The first few sounds mesmerized my audience.

"King Lister, Princesses, lords, ladies...there is no way I can explain the great honor being bestowed upon me. Princess Ina is every man's dream. Never will one tire of the variety of beauty that she possesses..."

I let my words die out, and I began to sing the ballad I had struggled to compose so perfectly. I sang of a man in love with a remarkable creature that was able to change into so many women that he never tired of her beauty. The King's subjects hung on to my every word, and Princess Ina grew more and more lovely as her confidence in her own worth blossomed.

My song subtly changed, telling of a stranger coming into that kingdom and stealing the love of the beautiful creature and taking her away from her home and her country. I could feel the idea taking hold and the crowd getting restless. I sang the last refrain again, loudly, and ended with a flurry of music from my lute.

The banquet ended in an ugly mood, and I slipped off to my room. The band of brave knights had gathered around King Lister, and I noticed Princess Annabella and Princess Rowena sitting with bewildered expressions on their beautiful faces. It only enhanced their loveliness more.

Dawn had just made its way into my bed chamber when there was a knock at my door. A page beckoned me to follow him to King Lister's chambers.

"Ra-me, brave troubadour, wizard composer of songs, I must talk with you." This was the way he started our conversation. "My subjects are not in favor of Princess Ina marrying a stranger. The brave knights that failed to rescue my daughter want another chance, and Princess Ina consents for me to give them another chance. They propose a joust with the winner becoming Princess Ina's husband and living forever here in Parkingham. Will you release me from my promise to you?"

"But King Lister..." I feigned shock.

"I know, lad, but you will not only be performing for the wedding; but I shall want you to compose and perform throughout the two weeks of the joust. And I will give you twice the gold that I offered you for the wedding, plus twice as much as you usually get for working a joust. You are young with so much of the world to see. You aren't ready to stay in Parkingham for the rest of your life." He urged me persuasively, and I relented graciously.

What a time we had at the joust. I was at my best. I achieved new heights in lyrics, and my instruments fairly played themselves.

Right after the wedding, I left with my heart, fortune, and head intact. I had a scroll from King Lister, recommending my qualifications to anyone needing a troubadour for any occasion.

And, Falstaff, I intend to live happily ever after.

Printed in the United States
By Bookmasters